THE GOOD-LUCK PENCIL

THE
GOOD-LUCK
PENCIL

DIANE STANLEY

pictures by
BRUCE DEGEN

Four Winds Press

Macmillan Publishing Company
866 Third Avenue, New York, N.Y. 10022
Collier Macmillan Canada, Inc.

Printed in the United States of America
10 9 8 7 6 5 4 3 2

The text of this book is set in
14 pt. ITC Cheltenham Light.
The illustrations are preseparated, rendered in
pencil and paint, and reproduced in three colors.

Library of Congress Cataloging-in-Publication Data
Stanley, Diane.
The good-luck pencil.
Summary: A magic pencil which Mary Ann
discovers accidentally brings her more
good luck than she can handle.
[1. Pencils—Fiction. 2. Magic—Fiction]
I. Degen, Bruce, ill. II. Title.
PZ7.S7869Go 1986 [E] 85-13122
ISBN 0-02-786800-1

for
ELAINE SCOTT
who has a gift
for friendship

Mary Ann was sitting at the bus stop when she remembered her math.

"Oh, nuts!" she said. "I forgot to do it."

She got her math workbook out of her book bag. Then she began rummaging around in the bottom for a pencil. All she found was crumpled paper, gum wrappers, and some loose change.

"Oh, nuts!" she said. "Christine, can I borrow a pencil?"

Christine said, "I might be needing it in a minute." Christine didn't like to share her things.

Todd said, "There's a pencil on the ground right beside your foot."

Mary Ann picked it up.

"Great!" she said. "It still has a good point."

She began doing her math. The answers seemed to flow from the pencil all by themselves. Mary Ann couldn't believe it. She was finished before the bus arrived.

At school Mrs. Forbes said, "Mary Ann, I want to congratulate you. You made 100 on your math!"

It had never happened before. Mary Ann put her pencil in the side pocket of her book bag, where it would be safe. It was her good-luck pencil.

All day long Mary Ann couldn't do anything wrong. Everybody noticed it. She got so many compliments she grew pink around the ears.

That afternoon Mrs. Forbes assigned a composition. Each of them was to write a page about his or her family.

"Please don't just say that you have a mother and father and two brothers. Make it interesting. Tell me what your parents do. Tell me about your hobbies. Tell me about your travels. Make it interesting!"

"Oh, nuts!" said Mary Ann to Todd on the way home. "My father works in a hardware store. My mother stays home. We watch television. How interesting!"

"Yeah," said Todd. "If I walked into your house by mistake I might live there for a week and never know the difference. Every house on the block is exactly alike."

"I went to Waco on the bus to see my grandmother once," said Mary Ann. "Some travels!"

When Mary Ann got home her mother was waiting with milk and cookies.

"Did you ever consider being a ballerina?" she asked her mother.

"No, I never even considered it."

"Figures!" said Mary Ann, taking her milk and cookies into the living room.

She took out her good-luck pencil and began to write.

MY FAMILY

My mother is a world-famous ballerina. She dances all over the world. Right now she is in Paris, France. My father is an astronaut. We live in a big mansion with a swimming pool the size of a football field. In my spare time I am a world-champion piano player. There are always lots of reporters out on the lawn wanting to take our pictures and ask us questions. We have to wear dark glasses and slip out the back way to keep from being recognized. This summer I plan to climb Mt. Everest.

Mary Ann put down her good-luck pencil and sighed. "She can't say it isn't interesting, anyway."

When Mary Ann looked up from her paper she got a jolt.

"*Omygosh!*" she gasped. Her living room was transformed. It looked like a palace.

"*Muh-theeeeeeer!*" yelled Mary Ann.

The door opened and a stout lady in black entered.

"Your mother is in Paris, Mary Ann, as you well know. And it is not refined to shout."

"Where is my daddy?" asked Mary Ann, close to tears.

"Your father is orbiting the earth, of course, and he is very busy. Come, now. It is time to practice the piano."

Mary Ann followed the lady down a long hallway. At last they entered the music room.

"You will begin with the Mozart. And try to be a little more lyrical this time. Remember what the critics said after your last performance."

Mary Ann tried to be lyrical for two hours.

"Can I stop now?" she pleaded.

"Yes, you *may*," said the lady in black. "Now for the Bach. You are weakest in Bach."

Mary Ann played Bach for two more hours.

"That is enough for today," the lady said at last. "Now for your workout. You must build up your endurance for your climb this summer."

"Why did I have to put *that* part in?" groaned Mary Ann as they walked down another half mile of corridors, through the ballroom, the reception room, the blue parlour, the red parlour, and the exercise room until they reached the dressing room.

"When you have put on your bathing suit you should begin with the usual one hundred laps. Your exercise instructor will be here shortly."

Mary Ann swam and swam and swam. After a while her head was swimming. She got out of the pool. Her exercise instructor was getting the weights ready. Suddenly she had an idea.

She called the swimming-pool maid over.

"Would you please bring me the school composition and the yellow pencil I left in the living room? And hurry!" The maid scurried away and Mary Ann began lifting weights.

At last the maid arrived with the composition and the pencil on a silver tray.

"Take a break," Mary Ann said to the exercise instructor.

She crossed out every word of her composition. Then she turned the paper over and wrote.

MY FAMILY

My father works in a hardware store. He doesn't make a lot of money, but he has a great sense of humor. And he's always there when I need him. My mother never even thought about being a ballerina, but she helps me with my homework and gives me hugs and kisses, sometimes just for nothing. I went to Waco on a bus once, and my grandmother gave me tea out of a flowered teapot, even though I was only four.

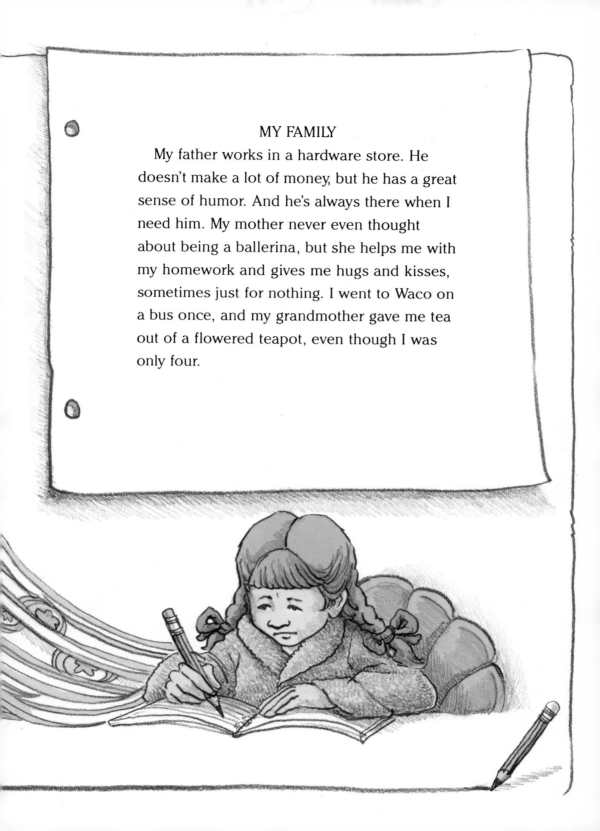

She was almost afraid to look up. When she did she let out a great sigh of relief.

"Mother!" she called.

"I'm in the garden, dear," came the sweet, familiar voice.

Mary Ann stood in the garden for a long time watching her mother plant little petunia seedlings.

At school the next day Mary Ann turned in her composition. Mrs. Forbes made her copy it over on a clean sheet of paper.

Mary Ann took out her good-luck pencil and stared at it for a long time. Then she walked over to the pencil sharpener and sharpened and sharpened until there was nothing left but a stub. The stub she threw away.

"Does anybody have a pencil I can borrow?" she asked.